MW00873682

BEYOND MY LABEL

Copyright

Copyright © 2020 by Kalynda Boyd
All rights reserved. This book or any portion thereofmay not be reproduced or used in any manner whatsoever without the express written permission of the publisher except for the use of brief quotations in a book review.

Printed in the United States of America

ISBN 9781087908120

Orders by U.S. trade bookstores and wholesalers. Please contact K. Boyd at boydkalynda6@gmail.com

Dedication

This book is dedicated to all the parents in the world that have a child with a disability. Finding out that your child will be labeled with a disability is not the easiest thing to accept but what you do with that information and how you handle the situation determines how you will both see and help your child thrive in this world.

My hope for this book is to help you to not fall victim to the cant's and don'ts that doctors and people may tell you about your child and to inspire you to just believe that God created a beautiful human being beyond the label your child may carry.

On a sunny afternoon after a very long work day, a vision came to Debbie of starting a business called Teenie Weenie Boutique!

With so much excitement Debbie rushed to her daughters school to share the news.

Debbie hopped out of the car and ran to the school doors, just for Mona's teacher to greet her with news of her own.

"Based upon today's assesment and development charts, Mona is showing signs of being nonverbal, but please do not fret."

Mona's teachers described that during the assessment Mona avoided eye contact when playing with other children and adults, displayed unusual facial expressions that don't match with what is being said, and makes very few gestures (such as pointing) or communicating what she wants and needs.

Mom didn't know how to handle the news she just received so she gathered up her daughter and all of her things and went on her way.

After arriving home Mona's mom still had much joy about her big idea that while Mona was playing with her toys mom told "Mona, I'm going to open up a kid's store and call it Teenie Weenie Boutique."

The two laughed and smiled from ear to ear, cheek to cheek.

Mom didn't let the news from Mona's school keep her down. She knew that no matter what, Mona would always make her proud.

After a busy day of work and Mona's speech
therapy, it was finally time to go home and get
dinner ready and prepare for the next day as well
as fill orders for the boutique.

When everything was all clean and put away,
and Mona was in bed, that's when mom
loved to create her socks and bows
because that's when all her
creativity would come
alive in her mind.

Just when mom was designing a pair of socks she looked up and saw two little brown eyes peeking from around the corner.

"Mona have you been there the whole time watching me make these socks and bows."
Mona nodded and smiled.

"Ok back to bed we go."
After a trip to the bathroom and a sweet goodnight kiss, mom tucked Mona back into bed and got back to business.

Just when Mom thought that Mona was asleep she heard a noise, so she got up to see what it was. She tip-toed over to see what Mona was up to.

She slowly opened the door to Mona's bedroom and was amazed at what she saw and thought " Oh how could this be"...

Mona had created her very own Teenie
Weenie Boutique in her room. Mona danced
around with her magical socks, bows lighting
up, as mom stood there in shock.

Just when mom was about to leave she bumped into the door, and Mona looked up and smiled as if to say see Mom I Can Do It Too was beaming from her brown eyes.

It was so amazing to see that even though Mona is not able to speak, she was able to observe, imitate, and succeed.

Things might not always turn out how they
seem, but with love and support
EVERY child can live out
their dreams.

"As special needs parents we don't have the power to make life "fair" but we do have the power to make life joyful."

For more help on how to deal with children with disabilities here are some PARENT RESOURCES.

- Parent to Parent USA.
- National Youth Leadership Network.
- National Collaborative on Workforce and Disability for Youth.
- The M.O.R.G.A.N. Project.
- Federation for Children With Special Needs.
- Family Voices.
- Council for Exceptional Children.
- Disabled Sports USA.

Beyond My Label is a book that is written to inspire parents with children with disabilities. We have to dismantle the stigmas of children with labels and disabilities and focus on helping them be the best they can be. Be inspired, Be moved and Be encouraged because all things work for the greater good.

CPSIA information can be obtained
at www.ICGtesting.com
Printed in the USA
LVHW071917251020
669603LV00017BB/348